not a rabbit!

A division of Hachette Children's Books

‘Guess what!’
says Wibbly Pig.
‘Big Pig’s sister’s
friend is getting
a new pet
today!’

It is true. Big Pig’s sister’s friend is off to the

pet shop with her pocket money.

'What do you think
she'll choose?' says
Scruffy Pig. 'I bet it will
be something boring.
Something really boring,
like a hamster. . .

or a goldfish. . .

or a **rabbit!**

Yes, that's what
she'll choose,
a **rabbit!**'

'Oh no, not a **rabbit!**'

'If you could choose,' says Wibbly Pig. 'If you could choose anything, anything at all, what would **YOU** choose?'

'Anything at all?' says Scruffy Pig.

'Anything,
except a rabbit.'

'I'd choose an
elephant!
We could have
a water fight
with an elephant!

You can't
do **that** with
a rabbit!'

'I'd have a **bear!**
Bears are best.
Especially polar bears!
Much better than
a rabbit!'

'It would be
cool to have a
kangaroo!

Tiny Pig could
go for a ride
in the pouch!

You can't do **that**
with a rabbit!'

'We could have
giraffes!
We could see for
miles on a
giraffe!'

'You can't
do that
with a rabbit
either.'

'Or what about a **dolphin**!'

'I bet she won't
choose anything
like **this!**'
says Scruffy Pig.

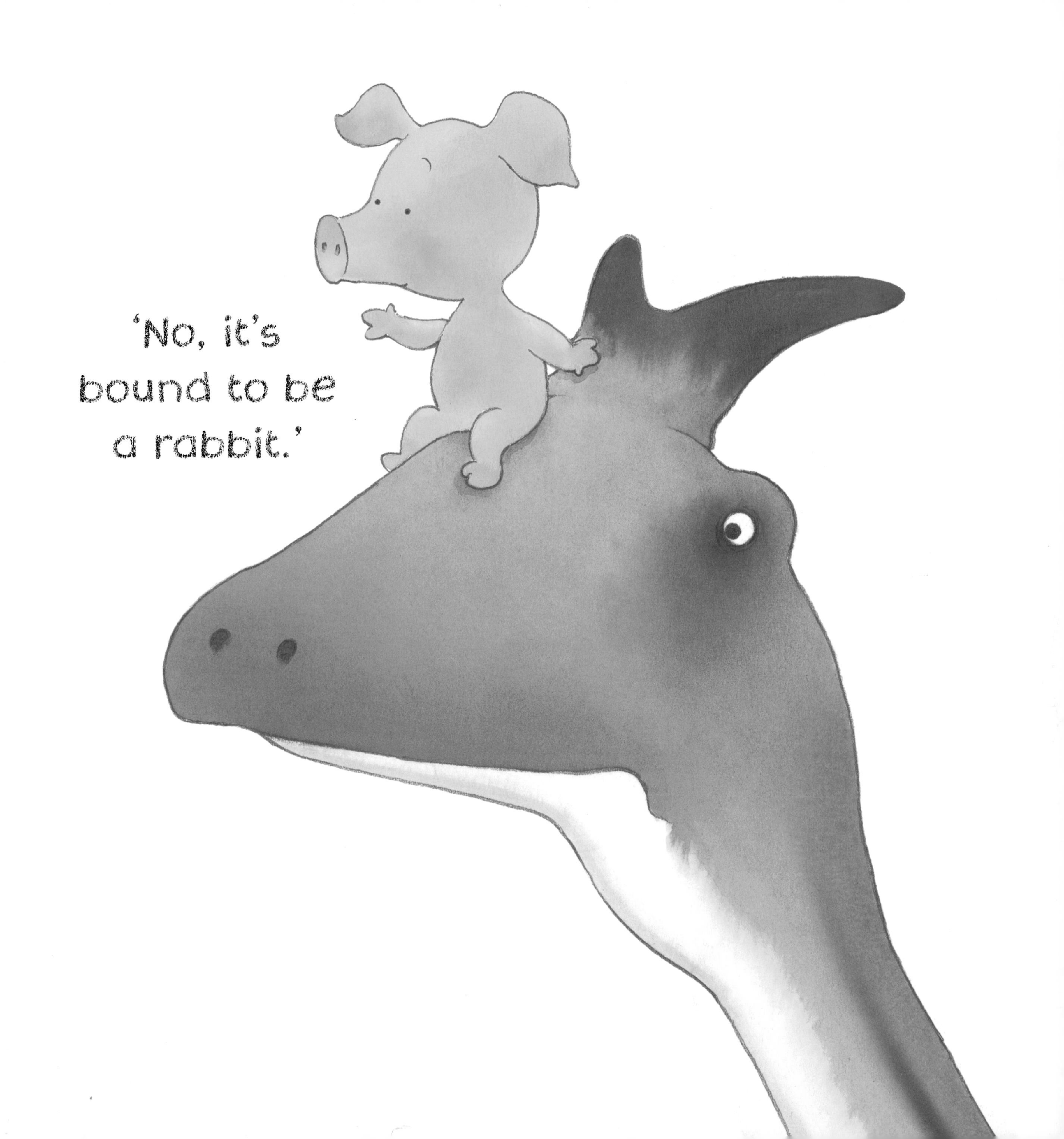

'No, it's
bound to be
a rabbit.'

And sure enough,
when Big Pig's sister's
friend comes back from
the pet shop she has a large,
brown and white. . .

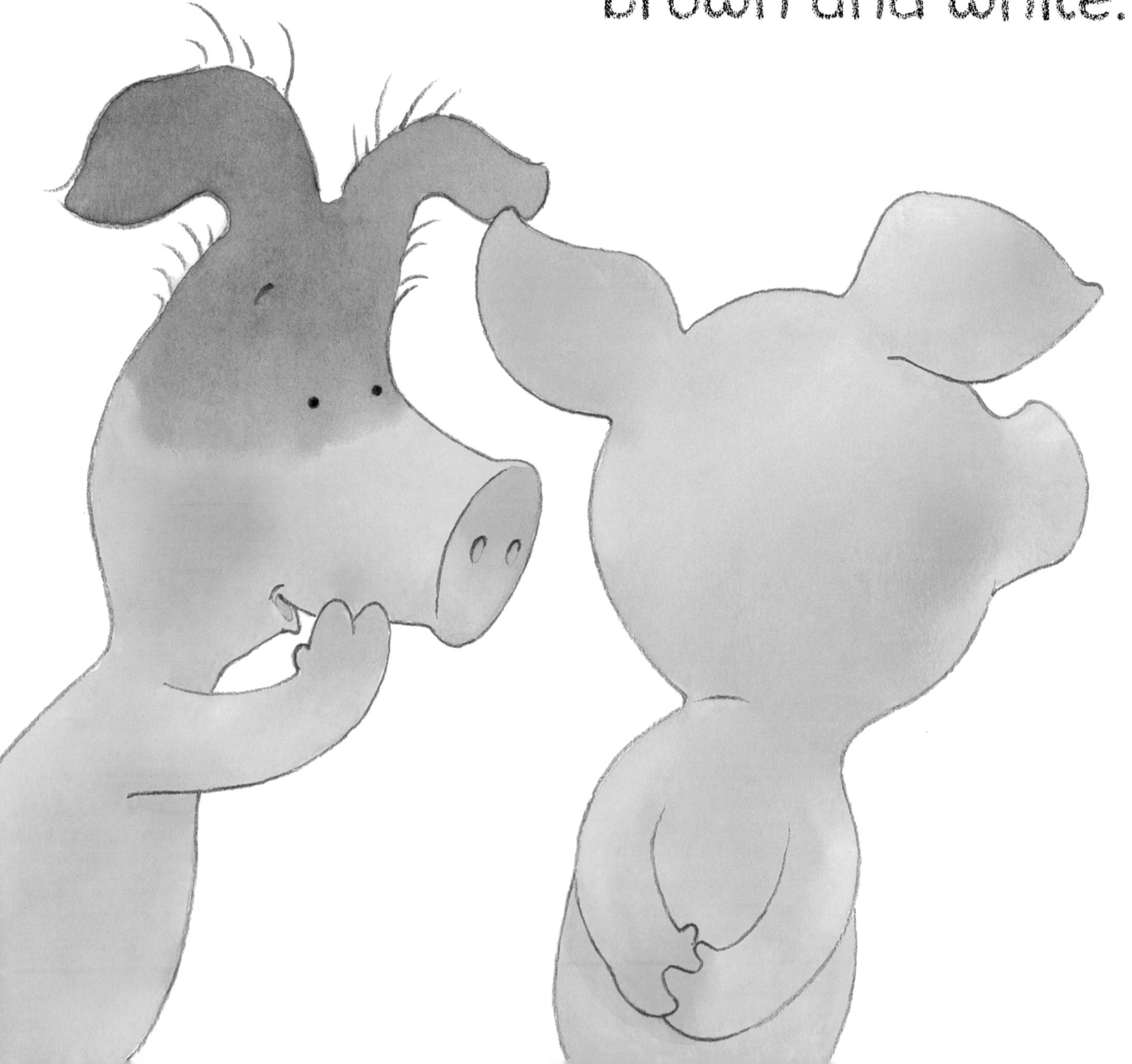

. . .rabbit.

'Thought so,' says Wibbly Pig.

'Boring!' whispers Scruffy Pig.

But,

the rabbit hops onto
Scruffy Pig's lap.
It licks his face.

(He forgets about the elephant.)

Then it licks Wibbly.

(He forgets about the polar bear and the kangaroo.)

The rabbit cleans its ears.

(They forget
all about the giraffe,
the dolphin
and the dinosaurs.)

The rabbit runs three times round Wibbly Pig and thumps the floor with its foot.

Thump!

Thump!

Thump!

'How much do rabbits cost?' says Wibbly Pig.

'It's really cute!'
says Scruffy Pig.

'Yes it is!'
says Big Pig's sister's
friend, very proudly. . .

'And he can do
two kinds
of poo,
too!'